Zen Shorts

By Jon J Muth

SCHOLASTIC PRESS • NEW YORK

SCHOLASTIC PRESS

LIBRARY OF CONGRESS CATALOGING-IN-PUBLICATION DATA

Muth, Jon J

Zen shorts / by Jon Muth ; illustrated by Jon Muth. — 1st ed.   p. cm.

Summary: When Stillwater the bear moves into the neighborhood, the stories he tells to three siblings teach them to look at the world in new ways.

ISBN 0-439-33911-1

[1. Bears—Fiction. 2. Brothers and sisters—Fiction. 3. Storytelling—Fiction.] I. Title.   PZ7.M97274 Ze 2005

[E]—dc22   2003020471

10 9 8 7 6   06 07 08 09

Printed in Mexico 49   First edition, March 2005

The artwork was created with watercolor and ink.

The text is set in 17-point Monotype Fournier

Book design by David Saylor

ACKNOWLEDGMENTS

Despite my best efforts to get in my own way, my great friends Dianne Hess and David Saylor have graciously cleared the path once more.

I offer humble thanks to the inspiration of Rafe Martin and Jack Kornfield, wonderful storytellers.

Thank you to B, N, A, and the newest and youngest member of my modeling staff, Karl.

For all of the various primary sources of the Zen stories, I offer a deep *gassho*-bow.

For Ballard Borich

the Giant Panda I've often found dancing on my porch

"MICHAEL! There's a bear outside!" said Karl.

"A what?" called Michael.

"A bear. He's really big. And he's in the backyard."

"What's he doing?" Michael asked.

"He's sitting. He has an umbrella," said Karl.

"An umbrella?"

By the time the boys got outside, their sister, Addy, was already talking with him.

"I'm sorry for arriving unannounced," said the bear. "The wind carried my umbrella all the way from my backyard to your backyard. I thought I would retrieve it before it became a nuisance." He spoke with a slight panda accent.

Michael introduced himself. Then Addy introduced Karl because Karl was shy around bears he didn't know.

And this is how Addy, Michael, and Karl met Stillwater.

The next day, Addy went to have tea with Stillwater.

"Hello?" Addy said as she stepped inside.

"Come in! Come in!" a faraway voice called.

Then she heard the voice say, "Oh, yes . . . Come out! Come out!"

Stillwater was in the backyard.

He was in a tent.

"This is a birthday present from my Uncle Ry," Stillwater said.
"He always gives presents on his birthday, to celebrate the day he was
born. I like it so much, that I'm not staying in my house right now."
Stillwater invited Addy to sit with him.

"You brought me some cake!" said Stillwater. "That was very nice of you. Is it *your* birthday?" he asked.

"No," said Addy.

"It's not mine, either," said Stillwater. "But let me give you a gift for my uncle's birthday. I will tell you a story."

Uncle Ry and the Moon

MY UNCLE RY lived alone in a small house up in the hills. He didn't own many things. He lived a simple life.

One evening, he discovered he had a visitor. A robber had broken into the house and was rummaging through my uncle's few belongings.

The robber didn't notice Uncle Ry, and when my uncle said "Hello," the robber was so startled he almost fell down.

My uncle smiled at the robber and shook his hand.

"Welcome! Welcome! How nice of you to visit!"

The robber opened his mouth to speak, but he couldn't think of anything to say.

Because Ry never lets anyone leave empty-handed, he looked around the tiny hut for a gift for the robber. But there was nothing to give. The robber began to back toward the door. He wanted to leave.

At last, Uncle Ry knew what to do.

He took off his only robe, which was old and tattered. "Here," he said. "Please take this."

The robber thought my uncle was crazy. He took the robe, dashed out the door, and escaped into the night.

My uncle sat and looked at the moon, its silvery light spilling over the mountains, making all things quietly beautiful.

"Poor man," lamented my uncle. "All I had to give him was my tattered robe. If only I could have given him this wonderful moon."

"Your uncle sounds nice," said Addy. "I don't think I could have given away my only robe."

"I know how that is," said Stillwater. "But there's always the moon."

"That was a good story," said Addy.

"Thank you," said Stillwater. "And this is good cake."

"Thanks," said Addy. "I made it myself."

The next day, Michael went to see Stillwater.

"Here I am!" Stillwater called from the tree.

"Can I come up?" asked Michael.

"If you are careful," said Stillwater.

"What if *we* could fly?" said Michael.

"We could cast shadows on clouds," said Stillwater.

"But what if we fell?" said Michael.

"If we fell, we might break something," said Stillwater.

"That would be bad," said Michael.

"Maybe," said Stillwater.

"Maybe?" asked Michael.

The Farmer's Luck

THERE WAS ONCE an old farmer who had worked his crops for many years.

One day, his horse ran away. Upon hearing the news, his neighbors came to visit.

"Such bad luck," they said sympathetically.

"Maybe," the farmer replied.

The next morning the horse returned, bringing with it two other wild horses.

"Such good luck!" the neighbors exclaimed.

"Maybe," replied the farmer.

The following day, his son tried to ride one of the untamed horses, was thrown off, and broke his leg.

Again, the neighbors came to offer their sympathy on his misfortune.

"Such bad luck," they said.

"Maybe," answered the farmer.

The day after that, military officials came to the village to draft young men into the army to fight in a war. Seeing that the son's leg was broken, they passed him by.

"Such good luck!" cried the neighbors.

"Maybe," said the farmer.

"I get it," said Michael. "Maybe good luck and bad luck are all mixed up. You never know what will happen next."

"Yes," Stillwater agreed. "You never know."

The day after that, Karl went to visit Stillwater.

"Michael said I couldn't bring over our stuff to go swimming. I'm mad at Michael. He's always telling me what to do. So I brought *everything*!"

"Hmmm," said Stillwater. "It's a little pool. I don't know if all those things will fit."

"Let's see!" Karl said.

"Let's see," said Stillwater.

Stillwater looked at the pool.

"The things can go swimming, but we can't," he said.

"I brought too much stuff," said Karl.

"That's okay," said Stillwater. "I'll help you carry it home later."

"Why does Michael always have to tell me what to do?" Karl said.

"If he were here, I would climb up really high . . .

. . . and I would jump on him like this . . .

. . . and I'd do a big SMASH, like this!"

Later, Karl and Stillwater had tea.

"Karl," said Stillwater. "You spent the whole day being angry with Michael. Did you notice how much fun *we* had?"

Karl watched the steam rise from his cup.

"I'm sorry I brought all this stuff," Karl said.

"You don't need to be sorry," said Stillwater.
"Right now, you need to carry. Hold on tight,
and I will tell you a story."

A Heavy Load

TWO TRAVELING MONKS reached a town where
there was a young woman waiting to step out of her
sedan chair. The rains had made deep puddles and
she couldn't step across without spoiling her silken
robes. She stood there, looking very cross
and impatient. She was scolding her
attendants. They had nowhere to
place the packages they held for
her, so they couldn't help her
across the puddle.

The younger monk noticed the woman, said nothing, and walked by. The older monk quickly picked her up and put her on his back, transported her across the water, and put her down on the other side. She didn't thank the older monk, she just shoved him out of the way and departed.

As they continued on their way, the young monk was
brooding and preoccupied. After several hours, unable to
hold his silence, he spoke out. "That woman back there
was very selfish and rude, but you picked her up on your
back and carried her! Then she didn't even thank you!"

"I set the woman down hours
ago," the older monk replied.
"Why are *you* still carrying her?"

"Do you think you have carried it long enough?" asked Stillwater.

"Yes," said Karl.

"Good," said Stillwater.

And this is how Addy, Michael, Karl — and Stillwater — became friends.

Author's Note

WHAT IS ZEN?

Zen is a Japanese word that simply means meditation. In Zen, the teachings of the Buddha have always been passed down from teacher to student.

The Buddha's method of meditation was to sit very still, yet remain completely alert, allowing first one thought and then another to rise and pass away, holding on to none of them.

When you look into a pool of water, if the water is still, you can see the moon reflected. If the water is agitated, the moon is fragmented and scattered. It is harder to see the true moon. Our minds are like that. When our minds are agitated, we cannot see the true world.

Stillwater's name came from this. His character is based partly on the Zen artist/teacher SENGAI GIBBON (1750-1838), whose drawings were used as gentle teaching tools. He was known for his humor and unorthodox teaching style. Uncle Ry is based on RYOKAN TAIGU (1758-1831). He was one of Japan's best-loved poets.

"Zen shorts" are short meditations — ideas to puzzle over — tools which hone our ability to act with intuition. They have no goal, but they often challenge us to reexamine our habits, desires, concepts, and fears.

The stories, "Uncle Ry and the Moon" and "A Heavy Load," come from Zen Buddhist literature which has been passed along for centuries. The story of "The Farmer's Luck" has roots going back to Taoism, which is several thousand years old. There are many versions of these stories. I have chosen the ones that I feel speak best to the youngest audience.